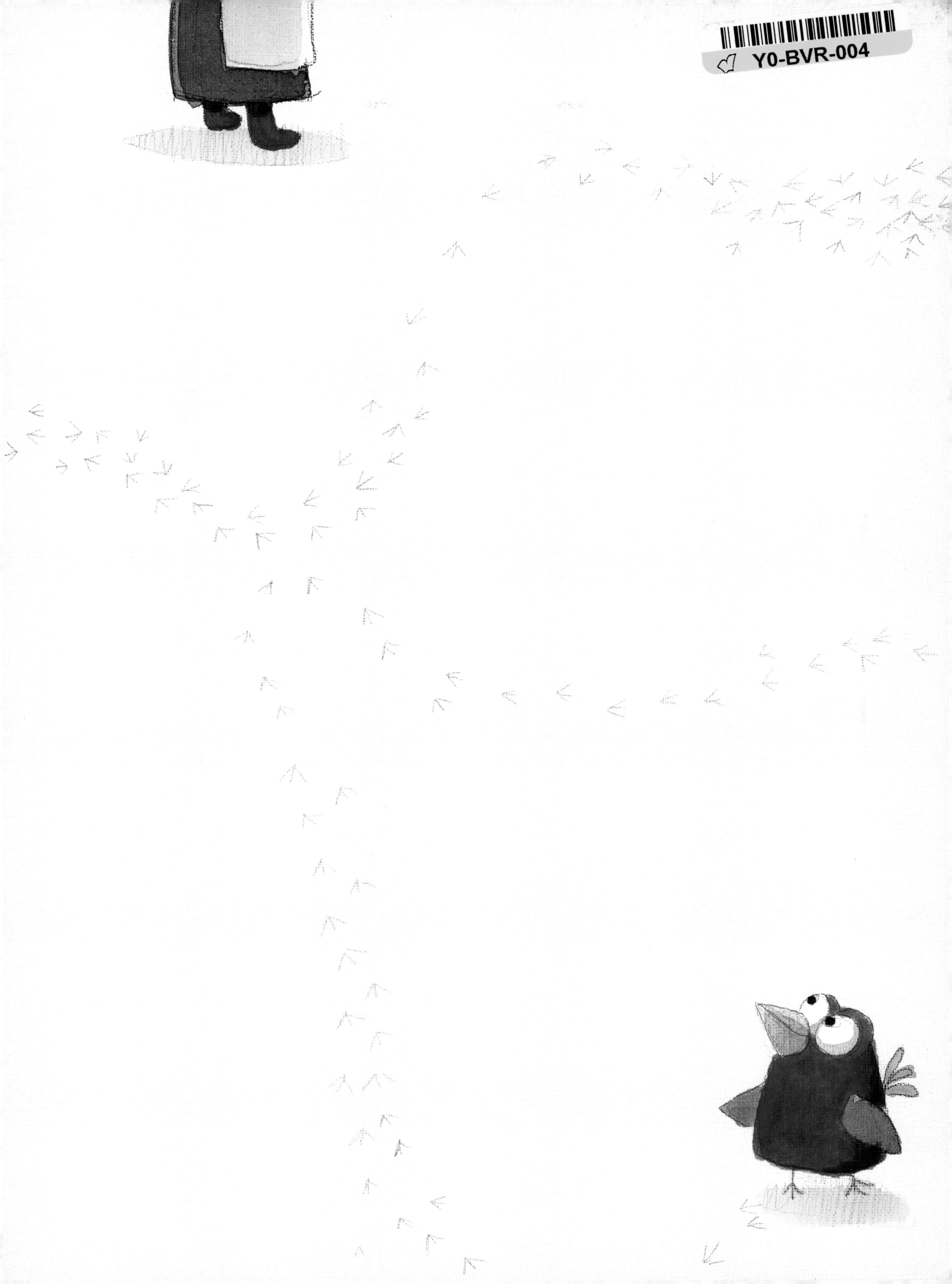

© for the original French edition: L'Élan vert, Paris, 2007
Original French title: Un Oiseau en hiver

© for the English edition: Prestel Verlag,
Munich · London · New York, 2011

Photo credit: Pieter Bruegel the Elder, The Hunters in the Snow (January),
1565 © Photo: Bridgeman

The Deutsche Nationalbibliothek lists this publication in the
Deutsche Nationalbibliografie; detailed bibliographic information
is available at http://dnb.d-nb.de

Prestel Verlag, Munich
A member of Random House GmbH
http://www.prestel.com

English translation: Cynthia Hall, Stephanskirchen

Editing: Brad Finger
Layout: Meike Sellier, Eching
Production: Franziska Creutzburg
Printing and binding: Tlačiarne BB, spol. s.r.o.
Printed in Slovakia.

FSC
MIX
From responsible
sources
FSC® C022120
www.fsc.org

Verlagsgruppe Random House FSC-DEU-0100
The FSC-certified paper LuxoSamt
is produced by mill Sappi, Biberist, Schweiz.

ISBN 978-3-7913-7080-4

A Bird in Winter

Inspired by a painting by Pieter Bruegel

Text by Hélène Kérillis

Illustrations by Stéphane Girel

PRESTEL

Munich · London · New York

Mayken is only eight years old, but she has to help
her mother in the inn.
Every day she must follow her mother's orders:
"Mayken, another jug of wine for the hunters!"
"Mayken, a bowl of soup for the cloth merchant!"
"Mayken, a slab of bacon for the doctor!"

Whenever she has time, Mayken gazes out the window.
Here she can forget the noisy life of the inn.

It's wintertime, and outside the snow
has swallowed up every sound.
In the sky, black birds pass by
above the white landscape.
Or they sit on branches, motionless and silent,
and dream of flying.
Mayken, too, wishes she could fly away.

Today is Sunday, Mayken's day to play on the ice.
The whole village has gathered there.
Children spin tops, play ice hockey,
or pull each other on sleds.
Mayken loves to feel the wind on her face
as she darts across the ice on her skates.
This is just how a bird in the sky must feel!

Ding dong! Ding dong! The village bells begin to ring.
Four o'clock already! Mayken has to rush home; she's late!
The path over the hill is shorter than the one along the street.
The hill is steep, though, and she has to go by the house of
the trapper, the scariest man in the village! If only she could
disappear into the landscape, like a shadow, and pass by unseen.
Suddenly the door is flung open and a dark figure shakes
his fist at her. "I'll teach you to snoop around here,"
the trapper shouts.

Mayken runs away terrified. She stumbles in the
deep snow, falls, and finally lands at the bottom
of the hill, covered with snow from head to foot.
In the bushes that break her fall, something seems
to stir quite close to her. Mayken holds her breath.
Out of the branches appears a small claw … a beak …

A bird! One of his wings is hanging limp, and he can no longer
fly. He can only hobble forward on his skinny legs. Surely the
trapper is to blame! Mayken carefully draws the little animal near.
"I'll nurse you back to health," she whispers. "Come with me!"
The bird lets Mayken take him in her hand.
But where will she keep him? Definitely not in the inn...
the hunters and their dogs are always coming and going.

Evening comes quickly, and Mayken arrives home late.
Now she must listen to her mother's scolding.
But all night long, Mayken thinks only about the little bird.
She has hidden him in the old mill!

As the sun arises the next morning, Mayken slips out of the inn
to bring her bird some food. Her path leads her to the river,
where she walks along the bank. Then she notices someone
crossing over the bridge above. Time to take cover behind a pier!

When the stranger is out of sight, Mayken quickly runs
to her hiding place in the old mill. The bird is still there!
Mayken takes the animal outside, underneath the wooden steps.
She gently strokes her little friend's pounding chest.
Even though Mayken has set its tiny wing, the bird still
is not strong enough to fly away. The girl reaches into her apron
and takes out a handful of grain that she stole from the henhouse.

Soon the village begins to stir, and Mayken has
to return home. But before she can leave her hiding place,
voices begin to approach.
"Now it's my turn!," one declares.
"No!," demands the other. "You still have to pull a little longer!"

Mayken looks out between the steps and sees two little children
and their father. They're playing right in front of the mill!
How can she leave unnoticed and get home on time?
If she's late again, she's sure to get a spanking …
or maybe even the whip!
The two children run across the ice, laughing.
But the father wants to move on, and the family begins to argue.
Mayken seizes her chance to run!

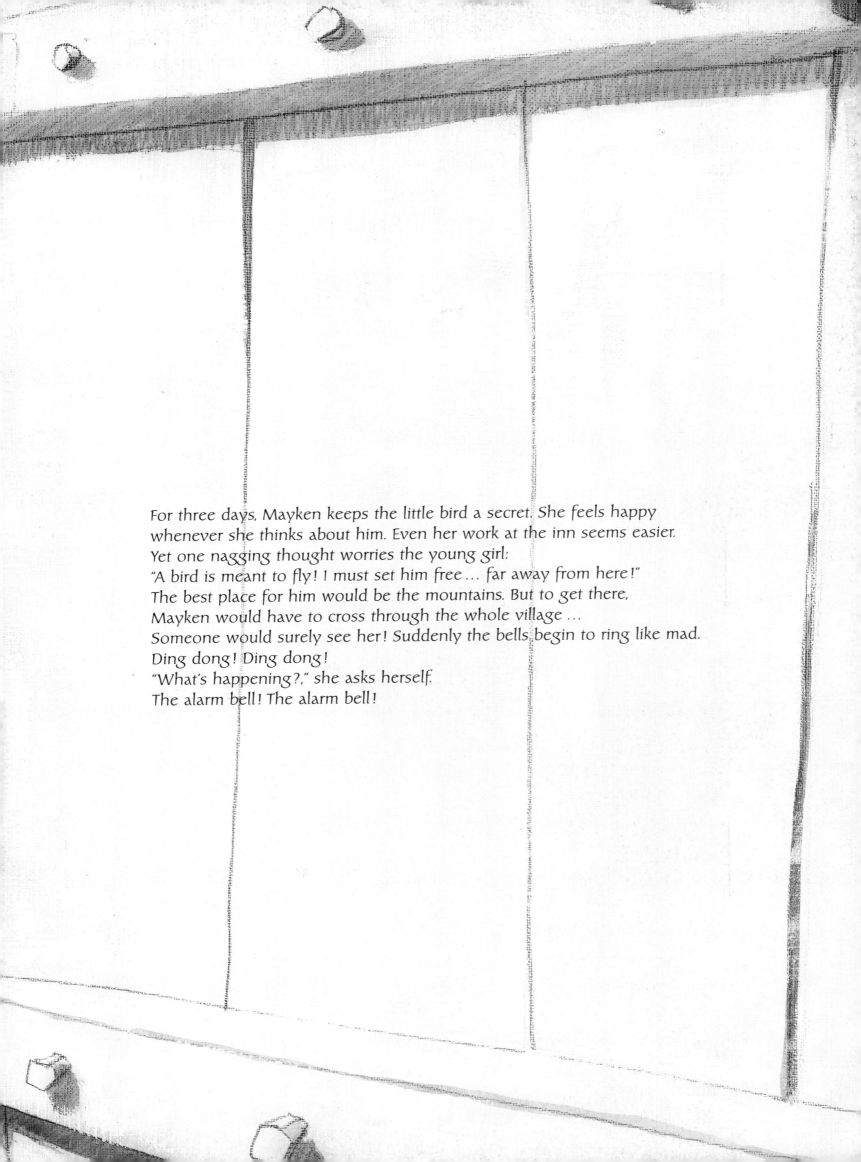

For three days, Mayken keeps the little bird a secret. She feels happy
whenever she thinks about him. Even her work at the inn seems easier.
Yet one nagging thought worries the young girl:
"A bird is meant to fly! I must set him free... far away from here!"
The best place for him would be the mountains. But to get there,
Mayken would have to cross through the whole village...
Someone would surely see her! Suddenly the bells begin to ring like mad.
Ding dong! Ding dong!
"What's happening?," she asks herself.
The alarm bell! The alarm bell!

The guests rush out from the inn and into the street!
"Fire! Fire!," they scream.
Mayken pushes her way between the frightened
townspeople. At the other end of the village,
she sees a chimney in flames. Everyone runs
towards the burning house, quickly emptying
the village streets. Now the girl can return safely
to her friend!

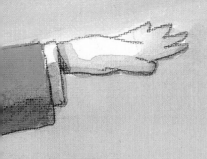

Mayken runs to the mill and fetches the little bird from
its hiding place. Eagerly, the two companions begin a journey
to find the bird its new home. They cross the empty village,
take the shortcut through the fields, and climb into the wintry
mountains. No one in the town has seen them.
The valley spreads out beneath Mayken, like a white tablecloth
dotted with tiny trees, houses, and ponds.
At last she finds a perfect spot for the bird, and she opens her coat
and sets the little one on her palm.
"Fly away!," Mayken says smiling. "Now you're home!"
The bird flaps its wings, its health restored, and it soars up
into the sky.

Mayken watches the bird for a while
and then starts back for home.
But something has changed.
The trees and bushes around her
seem strange. In the distance,
a dark wall is forming in the sky.
Night is falling! Mayken has lost her way!
Alone, tired, and bitterly cold,
the little girls sinks weakly
into the snow...

In the night, hunters find Mayken half frozen in the mountains.
The dogs have picked up her trail and saved her life.

Back at home, Mayken's punishment is hard … no skating on the lake
for a whole month! But the girl doesn't care. She lives like she's in a dream.

"Move over, Mayken! Don't just stand there in the way!"
Mayken moves aside so that her mother can stoke the fire.
The neighbors have arrived to help slaughter a pig.
But Mayken doesn't notice any of it. In her mind, she sees only
the beauty of the mountains and the endless sky,
where her little bird can now fly free once again …

Oil on wood
117 cm x 162 cm
1565
Kunsthistorisches
Museum, Vienna
(Austria)

Who

was Pieter Bruegel?

Pieter Bruegel—his name is also spelled Breugel, Breughel, or Brueghel—was a painter who lived most of his life in what is now Belgium. His son Pieter was also a famous painter, and this is why the father is often called Pieter Bruegel the Elder.

Why don't we know more about him?

Bruegel lived during the 1500s. At that time, even the greatest painters were often thought of as simple craftsmen—and not as famous artists. Because Bruegel did not achieve much fame in his own lifetime, we know little about him today.

Pieter Bruegel ca. 1525–1569